# THE SPELL OF THE YUKON.

**WRITTEN BY ROBERT SERVICE**

**ILLUSTRATED BY KAELAN PAULSON**

FOR MY BROTHER.

## The Spell of the Yukon

© 2021 by Kaelan Paulson

ISBN: 978-1-57833-776-7

**Written by Robert Service**
**Illustrated by Kaelan Paulson**

Published by

# K. Paulson Illustrations

736 Winterhaven St.
Anchorage, Alaska 99504
kgpspyguy@gmail.com


Distributed by

Todd Communications
611 E. 12th Ave., Suite 102
Anchorage, Alaska 99501-4603  U.S.A.
Phone: (907) 274-TODD (8633)
Fax: (907) 929-5550
sales@toddcom.com
WWW.ALASKABOOKSANDCALENDARS.COM

With other offices and warehouses in:
Juneau and Fairbanks, Alaska


First Printing April, 2021


Printed in China through **Alaska Print Brokers,** Anchorage, Alaska.

3

I WANTED THE GOLD, AND I SOUGHT IT;

I WANTED THE GOLD, AND I GOT IT--
CAME OUT WITH A FORTUNE LAST FALL,--
YET SOMEHOW LIFE'S NOT WHAT I THOUGHT IT,
AND SOMEHOW THE GOLD ISN'T ALL.

NO! THERE'S THE LAND. (HAVE YOU SEEN IT?) –
IT'S THE CUSSEDEST LAND THAT I KNOW,
FROM THE BIG, DIZZY MOUNTAINS THAT SCREEN IT
TO THE DEEP, DEATHLIKE VALLEYS BELOW.

SOME SAY GOD WAS TIRED WHEN HE MADE IT;
SOME SAY IT'S A FINE LAND TO SHUN;
MAYBE; BUT THERE'S SOME AS WOULD TRADE IT
FOR NO LAND ON EARTH--AND I'M ONE.

YOU COME TO GET RICH (DAMNED GOOD REASON);
YOU FEEL LIKE AN EXILE AT FIRST;
YOU HATE IT LIKE HELL FOR A SEASON,
AND THEN YOU ARE WORSE THAN THE WORST.

IT GRIPS YOU LIKE SOME KINDS OF SINNING;

IT TWISTS YOU FROM FOE TO A FRIEND;

IT SEEMS IT'S BEEN SINCE THE BEGINNING;

IT SEEMS IT WILL BE TO THE END.

I'VE STOOD IN SOME MIGHTY-MOUTHED HOLLOW-
THAT'S PLUMB-FULL OF HUSH TO THE BRIM;
I'VE WATCHED THE BIG, HUSKY SUN WALLOW
IN CRIMSON AND GOLD, AND GROW DIM,

TILL THE MOON SET THE PEARLY PEAKS GLEAMING,
AND THE STARS TUMBLED OUT, NECK AND CROP;
AND I'VE THOUGHT THAT I SURELY WAS DREAMING,
WITH THE PEACE O' THE WORLD PILED ON TOP.

THE SUMMER--NO SWEETER WAS EVER;
THE SUNSHINY WOODS ALL ATHRILL;
THE GRAYLING ALEAP IN THE RIVER,
THE BIGHORN ASLEEP ON THE HILL.

THE STRONG LIFE THAT NEVER KNOWS HARNESS;
THE WILDS WHERE THE CARIBOU CALL;
THE FRESHNESS, THE FREEDOM, THE FARNESS--
O GOD! HOW I'M STUCK ON IT ALL.

THE WINTER! THE BRIGHTNESS THAT BLINDS YOU,
THE WHITE LAND LOCKED TIGHT AS A DRUM,
THE COLD FEAR THAT FOLLOWS AND FINDS YOU,
THE SILENCE THAT BLUDGEONS YOU DUMB.

THE SNOWS THAT ARE OLDER THAN HISTORY,
THE WOODS WHERE THE WEIRD SHADOWS SLANT;
THE STILLNESS, THE MOONLIGHT, THE MYSTERY,
I'VE BADE 'EM GOOD-BY--BUT I CAN'T.

THERE'S A LAND WHERE THE MOUNTAINS ARE NAMELESS,
AND THE RIVERS ALL RUN GOD KNOWS WHERE;

THERE ARE HARDSHIPS THAT NOBODY RECKONS;
THERE ARE VALLEYS UNPEOPLED AND STILL;
THERE'S A LAND--OH, IT BECKONS AND BECKONS,
AND I WANT TO GO BACK--AND I WILL.

THEY'RE MAKING MY MONEY DIMINISH;

I'LL FIGHT--AND YOU BET IT'S NO SHAM-FIGHT;
IT'S HELL!--BUT I'VE BEEN THERE BEFORE;
AND IT'S BETTER THAN THIS BY A DAMSITE--
SO ME FOR THE YUKON ONCE MORE.

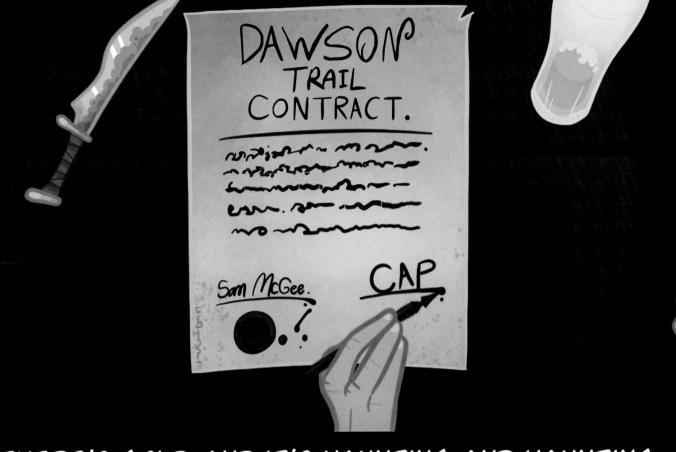

THERE'S GOLD, AND IT'S HAUNTING AND HAUNTING;
IT'S LURING ME ON AS OF OLD;
YET IT ISN'T THE GOLD THAT I'M WANTING
SO MUCH AS JUST FINDING THE GOLD.

IT'S THE GREAT, BIG, BROAD LAND 'WAY UP YONDER,
IT'S THE FORESTS WHERE SILENCE HAS LEASE;
IT'S THE BEAUTY THAT THRILLS ME WITH WONDER,
IT'S THE STILLNESS THAT FILLS ME WITH PEACE.

21

# About the Author:

Robert Service, "The Bard of the Yukon," was a British-born poet & writer whose
most famous works include
"The Cremation of Sam McGee"
"The Shooting of Dan McGrew"
and
"The Spell of the Yukon"
From his first published book, "Songs of a Sourdough."
His timeless poems are cherished by Alaskan
outdoorsmen to this day.

# ABOUT THE ARTIST:

KAELAN PAULSON IS AN ALASKAN AUTHOR AND ILLUSTRATOR.
BORN AND RAISED IN ANCHORAGE, AND COMPLETELY SELF
TAUGHT; HIS LOVE OF THE ALASKAN WILDERNESS GAVE BIRTH
TO THE VIBRANT STYLE THAT READERS OF ALL AGES ARE
GROWING TO KNOW AND LOVE.

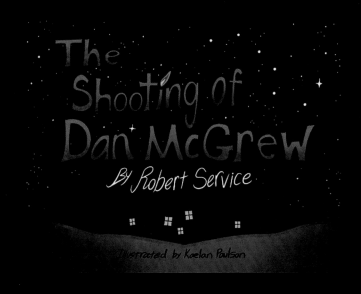

THE SHOOTING OF DAN MCGREW.

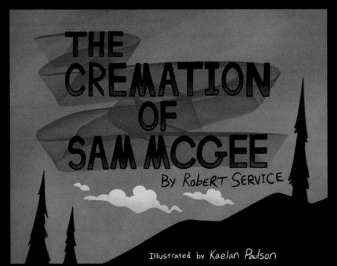

THE CREMATION OF SAM MCGEE.